...ggs is no ordinary dinosaur – he's an **ASTROSAUR!** Captain of the amazing spaceship DSS *Sauropod*, he goes on dangerous missions and fights evil – along with his faithful crew, Gipsy, Arx and Iggy.

For more astro-fun visit the website www.astrosaurs.co.uk

www.**kidsatrandomhouse**.co.uk

D0184209

Read all the adventures of
Teggs, Gipsy, Arx and Iggy!

Read the full set of Astrosaurs Academy adventures!

Find out more at www.astrosaurs.co.uk

Astrosaurs

THE T. REX INVASION

Steve Cole

Illustrated by Woody Fox

RED FOX

THE T. REX INVASION
A RED FOX BOOK 978 1 849 41403 6

First published in Great Britain by Red Fox,
an imprint of Random House Children's Books
A Random House Group Company

This edition published 2012

1 3 5 7 9 10 8 6 4 2

Text copyright © Steve Cole, 2012
Cover illustration and cards copyright © Dynamo Design, 2012
Map copyright © Charlie Fowkes and Steve Cole, 2005
Illustrations by Woody Fox copyright © Random House Children's Books, 2012

The right of Steve Cole to be identified as the author of this work has been asserted in
accordance with the Copyright, Designs and Patents Act 1988.

All rights reserved. No part of this publication may be reproduced, stored in a retrieval system,
or transmitted in any form or by any means, electronic, mechanical, photocopying, recording
or otherwise, without the prior permission of the publishers.

The Random House Group Limited supports the Forest Stewardship Council (FSC®), the
leading international forest certification organization. Our books carrying the FSC label are
printed on FSC®-certified paper. FSC is the only forest certification scheme endorsed by the
leading environmental organizations, including Greenpeace. Our paper procurement policy
can be found at www. www.randomhouse.co.uk/environment.

MIX
Paper from
responsible sources
FSC® C016897

Typeset in Bembo MT Schoolbook 16/20pt
by Falcon Oast Graphic Art Ltd.

Red Fox Books are published by Random House Children's Books,
61–63 Uxbridge Road, London W5 5SA

www.**kids**at**randomhouse**.co.uk
www.**randomhousebooks**.co.uk
www.**totallyrandombooks**.co.uk

Addresses for companies within The Random House Group Limited can
be found at: www.randomhouse.co.uk/offices.htm

THE RANDOM HOUSE GROUP Limited Reg. No. 954009

A CIP catalogue record for this book is available from the British Library.

Printed and bound in Great Britain by Great Britain
by CPI Bookmarque, Croydon, CR0 4TD

For Thomas Larkman –
winner of the Astrosaurs
Search For A Superfan
competition for his suggested
character, Tute

Northamptonshire Libraries & Information Services BD	
Askews & Holts	

WARNING!

THINK YOU KNOW ABOUT DINOSAURS?

THINK AGAIN!

The dinosaurs . . .

Big, stupid, lumbering reptiles. Right?

All they did was eat, sleep and roar a bit. Right?

Died out millions of years ago when a big meteor struck the Earth. Right?

Wrong!

The dinosaurs weren't stupid. They may have had small brains, but they used them well. They had big thoughts and big dreams.

By the time the meteor hit, the last dinosaurs had already left Earth for ever. Some breeds had discovered how to travel through space as early as the Triassic period, and were already enjoying a new life among the stars. No one has found evidence of dinosaur technology yet. But the first fossil bones were only unearthed in 1822, and new finds are being made all the time.

The proof is out there, buried in the ground.

And the dinosaurs live on, way out in space, even now. They've settled down in a place they call the Jurassic Quadrant and over the last sixty-five million years they've gone on evolving.

The dinosaurs we'll be meeting are

 part of a special group called the Dinosaur Space Service. Their job is to explore space, to go on exciting missions and to fight evil and protect the innocent!

These heroic herbivores are not just dinosaurs.

They are *astrosaurs*!

NOTE: The following story has been translated from secret Dinosaur Space Service records. Earthling dinosaur names are used throughout, although some changes have been made for easy reading. There's even a guide to help you pronounce the dinosaur names on the next page.

Talking Dinosaur!

How to say the prehistoric
names in this book . . .

STEGOSAURUS –
STEG-oh-SORE-us

IGUANODON –
ig-WHA-noh-don

HADROSAUR –
HAD-roh-SORE

DIMORPHODON –
die-MORF-oh-don

TRICERATOPS –
try-SERRA-tops

EGYPTOSAURUS –
ee-JIP-toh-SORE-us

TYRANNOSAURUS REX –
tye-RAN-oh-SORE-us REX

THE CREW OF THE DSS SAUROPOD

**CAPTAIN
TEGGS STEGOSAUR**

ARX ORANO,
FIRST OFFICER

GIPSY SAURINE,
COMMUNICATIONS
OFFICER

IGGY TOOTH,
CHIEF ENGINEER

Jurassic Quadrant

Ankylos Noxia

Steggos

Diplox

INDEPENDEN
DINOSAUR
ALLIANCE

Vegetarian

Sector

Squawk
Major

DSS
UNION OF
PLANETS

PTEROSAURIA

Corytho

Tri System  Lambeos

Iguanos

Aqua Minor

Geldos Cluster

Teerex
Major

Sphinx II

Olympus

TYRANNOSAUR
TERRITORIES

carnivore

Raptos

Planet Sixty

sector

THEROPOD EMPIRE

Megalos

Cryptos

vegmeat
zone

(neutral space)

EA REPTILE
SPACE

Pliosaur
Nurseries

Not to scale

THE
T. REX INVASION

Chapter One

THE TREASURE HUNTERS

"Woo-hoooooooo!"

yelled
Captain
Teggs
Stegosaur,
whizzing
across
the brilliant
green ocean on a

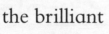

turbo-charged jet-ski. He laughed as a salty breeze blew all about him, soaking his red lifejacket. "I hate taking holidays – but I have to admit this is fun!"

"It sure is!" Iggy Tooth, a tough iguanodon, drew alongside him on

1

another jet-ski – then turned sharply away. "Come on, Captain. Race you back to shore!"

Teggs whooshed away after him. He and Iggy were astrosaurs – dinosaur astronauts, more used to shooting through the stars than over the sea. But their incredible spaceship, the *Sauropod*, was in the Galactic Garage for its ten-billion-mile service. It would take five days to complete, and so the whole crew had been sent on leave. Teggs had chosen their destination – the holiday world of Sphinx II . . .

The wind whistled past the spines on Teggs's back as he went even faster. But then the rockets on Iggy's jet-ski flared crimson, and with a surge of super-speed sent him hurtling up onto the shore, where he skidded to a stop in the sand.

"The winner!" Iggy punched the air. "Although, to be fair, I might have tinkered with my jet-ski's engines a *little* bit."

Teggs grinned as he swept up onto the beach. "I'd expect nothing less from the *Sauropod*'s Chief Engineer!"

At the mention of their ship, Iggy sighed. "I wish I could've stayed on board and helped the space mechanics fix her up."

"Don't start that again, Iggy Tooth," came a firm female voice from behind them. "You're as bad as the captain. You could both use a holiday."

"So you keep telling us!" Teggs smiled to see his communications officer, Gipsy Saurine, approaching with a tray of split-open coconuts. "Hi, Gipsy."

"I thought you dino-racers might like a drink." The stripy hadrosaur had swapped her usual red uniform for a blue swimsuit, and looked very relaxed. "So I brought coconut cocktails."

"How kind." Teggs quickly drained four coconuts, then swallowed the hard, hairy shells too. "Mmmm, delicious."

Gipsy frowned. "I see your stomach isn't taking a break!"

"Never!" Teggs shrugged off his lifejacket and patted his tum through his white T-shirt. He wasn't only the bravest dinosaur in space – he was the hungriest too.

"Thanks, Gipsy." Iggy drank the remaining coconut then took off his own lifejacket to reveal a bright Hawaiian shirt. "Have you seen Arx around?"

"Yes, what's our fine First Officer up to?" Teggs wondered.

"He's playing volleyball in the hotel pool with the alarm pterosaur." Gipsy pointed past the paved white plaza adjoining the beach, to where a bright green triceratops splashed with

a flying reptile in a beautiful lagoon. "Only trouble is, between his horns and her beak they keep bursting the ball!"

Teggs chuckled. "It's good to see everyone enjoying themselves." His crew were scattered all about the spotless grounds of the luxury hotel; from here he could see his pterosaur flight-team, the dimorphodon, playing weightless tennis in the zero-gravity courts . . . Alass the security chief was doing dino-gymnastics with her ankylosaur security guards in the open-air gym . . . the ship's cleaners were playing edible golf on a delicious grassy course . . .

And a boy dinosaur in white robes and a blue-and-gold headdress – who was NOT a member of the *Sauropod* crew – was striding purposefully along the beach towards Teggs and his friends.

"Captain," said Gipsy, "you never told us why you picked Sphinx II for our vacation."

"It wouldn't have anything to do with the fact that this was once a T. rex world, would it?" Iggy smiled. "Knowing the

6

captain, he's probably hoping there are a few of them still about to track down and capture. What better reason for coming could there be?"

"You're about to *meet* the reason." Teggs pointed to the approaching white-robed dinosaur. "Iggy, Gipsy, I'd like you to meet an old friend of mine from the planet Egyptus – Tute the treasure-hunter!"

"Teggsy, you old space-slug!" Tute charged up and hugged the stegosaurus. "How're you doing? It's been years! You're looking fat! Glad you could make it. And your friends!" He kissed Gipsy's hoof while slapping Iggy chummily on the back. "Who are you? I don't know! But if you're mates with old Teggsy you're all right by me."

Teggs quickly introduced his baffled friends. "Tute and I used to meet each year at school space camp," he explained. "He was the only dinosaur there who liked adventures as much as me!"

"So we became friends," Tute agreed. "But while Teggsy trained as an astrosaur, I studied ancient treasure-hunting! I've explored the whole Egyptus star system, digging up long-lost relics and searching out smugglers' gold . . ."

"How exciting!" Gipsy declared.

"This planet is at the edge of the Egyptus system, isn't it?" said Iggy, and Tute nodded. "Are you looking for treasure here?"

"Not any more. Because I've *found* it!" Tute pulled a satchel from under his white robes and held it upside down. Iggy and Gipsy gasped as huge gemstones came tumbling out.

Teggs went boggle-eyed. "That lot must be worth a fortune!"

"I'll say it is." Tute nodded proudly. "And I reckon it's just a taster of the treasure I'll find once I get inside this old T. rex pyramid I've found in the desert. It's got to be the find of the decade! Of the century! Of *for ever*!" He grinned. "So naturally, I spilled the beans to old Teggsy in a space-mail straight away."

Iggy crouched to admire a large, round ruby. "Why?"

"Because if I'm right about the riches there could be inside this T. rex temple," said Tute, "the T. rexes themselves might take an unhealthy interest."

"Members of the DSS will be needed to protect the pyramid." Teggs smiled. "So since we had nothing on for five days, I thought I'd catch up with my old pal and explore an ancient pyramid full of treasure! What holiday in the universe could top that?"

"How about one where your closest crewmates come along too?" Iggy angled hopefully. "We're up for it, aren't we, Gipsy?"

Gipsy nodded. "And I'm sure Arx will be too."

"The more the merrier!" Tute scooped up the jewels from the sand. "I'll bet there's so much treasure inside that pyramid it'll take loads of us to shift it . . ."

"I never heard of T. rexes building pyramids," said Gipsy. "Are you sure it's

theirs? Have you seen inside?"

"Well, no," Tute admitted. "I haven't been able to open the door yet. But it must be theirs. T. rexes were the first dinos ever to come to Sphinx II, and they left a thousand years ago."

Gipsy's eyes had grown wider. "But why did they leave?"

"No one knows for sure," said Tute. "T. rex history is kind of hazy – they keep eating their historians! But according to legend, five hundred T. rexes disappeared overnight and the rest fled the planet. Their rulers declared that Sphinx II was a cursed world. That's why the carnivores never came back!"

"It might have been cursed for them, but it's a plant-eaters' paradise." Iggy frowned. "Why didn't the T. rexes take their treasure with them? Why leave it all behind in a pyramid?"

"Perhaps we'll find out," said Teggs.

"Anyway, my space-car is parked outside the resort's main entrance," Tute told them. "Fetch your friend and meet me there as soon as you can, yeah?"

"Will do," called Teggs, grinning at Iggy and Gipsy. "Well, you heard Tute. Let's grab Arx – and get treasure-hunting!"

Chapter Two

SINISTER SENTRIES

Teggs, Gipsy and Iggy ran over to Arx and told him Tute's news. Arx was so excited he did a double backflip right out of the pool, and almost sent the alarm pterosaur flying!

"Of course, plant-eaters have only been holidaying on Sphinx II for a hundred years." Arx shook water from his horns. "Nine hundred years before that, T. rexes lived here. They were ruled by Lord Ganster, who was very clever by T. rex standards."

Gipsy scoffed. "You mean he could talk and eat at the same time?"

"No, he really *was* bright. And his followers thought he was fab. They did anything he said." Arx frowned. "It's so strange that they all vanished from this world and never came back. The T. rexes who ran away were teased by other carnivores for ages. They never talked about what happened."

"Good," squawked the alarm pterosaur. "I like meat eaters to keep their mouths closed!"

Teggs smiled. "Can you tell the rest of the crew where we've gone? I can't wait to get exploring!"

"I'll tell them," she replied, flapping away. "I'll tell them – SQUAWK!"

The astrosaurs hurried to the hotel gates. Just as they arrived, a large, rusty red planet-rover pulled up. "All aboard, me old mates!" called Tute through the driver's window. "Next stop, the pyramid of plunder!"

Teggs ushered his friends on board the chunky transport. "Hey, Tute, meet my fab friend Arx."

Tute beamed. "It's a pleasure, horn-head!"

"Likewise." Arx noticed the satchel full of gemstones hanging from Tute's seat. "Is that the treasure you've found?"

"Sure is." Tute steered the planet-rover up into the air and zoomed away.

16

"Funny thing is, they're different types of gem, but all the same size – and all perfectly round."

"Perfect full stop!" Gipsy grinned. "What amazing luck to discover an ancient treasure trove in all those miles of desert."

"It wasn't luck, Stripy, it was hard work!" Tute protested. "I was scanning Sphinx II's surface with special X-ray beams for months, looking for any traces of T. rex treasure in the sand. Finally I found the pyramid and managed to dig it out." He scowled. "Now, if only I could get inside the thing!"

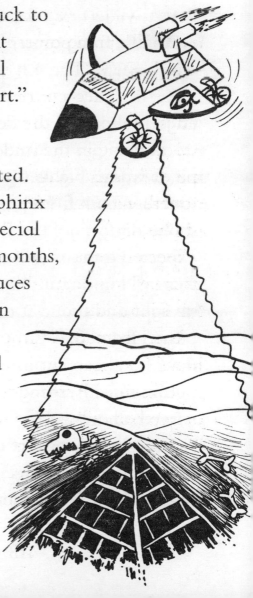

"I'm sure we'll find a way," said Teggs.

The journey took several hours, and Teggs fidgeted impatiently the whole time. There was nothing to see but the desert wilderness all around.

Finally, Tute pointed through the windscreen. "There it is – up ahead!"

As the space-car drew closer Teggs eagerly drank in the details. The pyramid stood alone in the middle of a huge pit. It was as big as four houses stuck together, built from pale stone that shone almost gold in the sunlight. He'd expected a thousand-year-old building to be old and crumbling but it stood so straight and proud it could easily have passed for new. A large rectangular door had been cut into one side of the pyramid, with strange signs and symbols carved all around it.

Tute parked a short distance away and led the astrosaurs outside. Nothing moved. Nothing made a sound. The

silence and the emptiness around them made Teggs feel a little uneasy.

"Bless my horns!" Arx peered at the pictures on the pyramid. "I had no idea T. rexes were so artistic."

"Or so rich." Gipsy picked up a ruby from the sand, identical in shape and size to the other jewels. "Why would they leave a fortune like this outside a sealed pyramid?"

Iggy shrugged. "Perhaps it's stuffed so full of treasure it's overflowing!"

"Possibly," said Arx thoughtfully. "Or perhaps there's another reason . . ."

Teggs banged on the door with his tail. "Seems pretty secure."

"It is," said Tute. "I've tried everything

– pushing, pulling, lifting, lowering, socking it with a super-shovel . . . but it won't budge an inch." He pulled a small white square from inside his robes. "I've got a blasting charge here – an explosion-in-a-box that *might* just crack the door open – but I don't want to risk damaging whatever's in there."

"Er, guys?" Gipsy gulped and pointed to the far side of the pyramid. "Perhaps we should ask *them* how to get in."

Teggs turned and gasped to find two towering creatures shambling into sight from round the corner. Walking on their hind legs, they were wrapped in filthy bandages from the tops of their heads to the tips of their tails. Their eyes glinted like dark jewels, and their skinny arms ended in dirty, jagged claws.

At the sight of Tute and the astrosaurs, they paused, staring intently.

"What *are* those things?" Iggy whispered.

Teggs grimaced. "They look like T. rexes to me."

"Not just any T. rexes." Tute was staring at the bandaged behemoths, transfixed. "*Mummy* T. rexes. Thousands of years ago, back home on Egyptus, they used to preserve the bodies of dead dinosaurs by wrapping them up, just like that."

"Only these mummies are very much alive," Arx pointed out.

"YOU," hissed one of the creatures in a voice like crunched-up ice-cubes. "You wish . . . to enter . . . the pyramid . . . ?"

"Never mind that," said Teggs. "This is a plant-eater world now — meat-eaters have no right to be here."

"Us have EVERY right," snarled the larger one. "This be OUR pyramid." Baring their teeth, the gruesome creatures stomped forward . . .

"You'd better stay back, Tute," Teggs warned his friend as the mummified monsters broke into a blundering charge. "The astrosaurs will handle this!" And with a super-strong sweep of his spiky tail, he tripped the closest creature.

"OOF!" the T. rex yelled as it fell to the sand with a crash.

Iggy quickly jumped on top of the carnivore's bandaged bonce. "Ha! That's one way to get *ahead*!"

Gipsy and Arx, meanwhile, took on the second T. rex. "Let's charge it from different directions," cried Arx. "It won't know which of us to fight first!"

But the still-standing mummy dodged their attack with surprising speed. Gipsy and Arx crashed into each other! Losing their balance, they tripped over the first

T. rex and knocked into Iggy and Teggs. With a chorus of cries, all four tumbled down together beside the pyramid door.

Teggs saw the second mummy drag its fallen comrade back to its feet, and braced himself to battle on. But the bandaged monsters turned from their prey and scrambled away up the sandy slope opposite.

"Weird," said Tute, scurrying forward
to help the astrosaurs. "They could've
rushed you while you recovered – so
why run away?"

"They're *not* running away." Gipsy
pointed. "They're running on the spot!"

Teggs realized she was right. The
wrapped-up 'rexes seemed to be doing
a strange kind of dance on the top
of the dune, their rear legs sending a
steadily thickening stream of
sand surging back down
the slope towards
Tute and the
astrosaurs ...

"It's a
landslide!" Teggs
yelled as the
dune collapsed
completely and
tons of sand swept
down all around
them. "Run for it!"

But the tide of golden grains was too fast for them. Within seconds, Teggs found himself up to his tummy in heavy sand. He couldn't move his legs. Grit blew into his eyes, blinding him. He heard his friends gasp and splutter beside him and tried to help them – but the sand's colossal weight was pressing down on his backplates, tightening around his scaly neck . . .

Chapter Three

SECRETS IN THE SAND

Suddenly – **Ba-BOOM!** A massive
explosion blasted through the desert
avalanche. The shockwave wrenched
Teggs free of his prison of sand, sent
him hurtling through the air until—
WHUMP! He slammed into the side of
the pyramid and just managed to cling
on. "Guys!" he shouted, blinking the sand
from his eyes. "Are you all OK?"

"Just about!" called Gipsy weakly from
somewhere below him.

Teggs found himself halfway up the
pyramid. Iggy was dangling from the
stonework just to his left, while Arx and
Gipsy were sprawled in drifts of sand by

the entrance. A huge crater had been blown in the ground close by, and Tute stood at the edge, panting for breath.

But of the dino-mummies there was now no sign.

"What happened?" groaned Iggy, starting to climb down.

"That blasting charge I brought along," said Tute shakily. "It must've fallen out of my robes when that sand-slide came down on us – and exploded under the pressure."

"We were lucky." Arx helped Gipsy to her feet. "The sand absorbed the explosion and the shockwaves set us free."

"And look . . ." Climbing down after Iggy, Teggs noticed a large rectangular slab sticking out of the sand opposite the pyramid doors. "We didn't know *that* was there before. It looks like some sort of sculpture."

"Wow!" Forgetting his shock and breathless with excitement, Tute ran up to it and brushed away more of the sand to reveal five small holes drilled in a straight line across the stone. "I've never seen anything like this with the other pyramids in the Egyptus system . . ."

"Those horrid T. rex things must've been standing on the sand above it," said Gipsy. "Were they zapped in that explosion?"

Arx shook his head. "There would be some trace of them left behind. They must've got away."

"Then we'd better get after them," said Teggs, bounding away up the steep sandy slope. "Gipsy, you stay with Tute in case they come back. Arx, Iggy – with me!"

Arx and Iggy followed their captain, ready to do battle. They split up and checked right around the pyramid. But there were no tracks and nothing to see.

Only the rolling desert
sands stretching out in
all directions.

"It's like they
just . . . disappeared!"
said Arx. "But how?"

"There's *one* place
they could've gone."
Teggs pointed to the
pyramid. "In there!" He led his friends
back down to Tute and Gipsy. "Could
there be a hidden entrance to this thing?"

"It's possible," Tute agreed.

Teggs nodded thoughtfully. "We should
get back to the resort and put out a
T. rex warning."

"Perhaps some of us should stay here
and keep watch for more mummies,"
said Arx.

"That's a good idea," said Teggs.
"Iggy, Gipsy, tell Alass and her security
guards to be ready for action and put
the dimorphodon on patrol. Then go to

31

Shuttle Alpha in the parking bay and contact the DSS. They must scan for carnivore ships."

"Right – those T. rex mummies must've got here somehow," said Iggy.

"We'll report back just as soon as we can," added Gipsy.

As Iggy and Gipsy raced away up the slope to the space-car, Tute suddenly leaped in the air. "I'VE GOT IT!" he boomed.

"Got what?" asked Teggs.

"This slab!" Tute's eyes were gleaming. "It's exactly the same shape and size as the door opposite. But it has five holes in it — holes that just happen to be the same size as all these gemstones lying around . . ." He stuck a round diamond into the first hole — it was a perfect fit. "See?"

Arx nodded. "I said there had to be a reason why there were so many jewels lying about. Perhaps they're here to help us open the door."

"Like a secret key, you mean?" said Tute.

"Five holes . . . and five different types of jewel," Teggs said slowly. "Diamonds, rubies, emeralds, sapphires and pearls."

"That might be it, Captain!" Arx stared around, excited. "Maybe, to open the door, we have to put the right jewels in the right holes in the right order."

"But how do we work out that order?" Tute asked. "It could take us weeks to try out all the possible patterns."

"Hang on," said Teggs. "If there's only space for five jewels, why leave so many more lying around out here? It's got to be a clue . . ."

"You're right." Arx thought hard. "Perhaps we have to count how many there are of each gemstone? The rarest gem goes in the first hole, the second-rarest gem goes in the second hole, and so on."

Tute beamed. "That's genius!"

"That's Arx," said Teggs proudly. "What are we waiting for? Let's try it out!"

Working at super-speed, Teggs, Arx and Tute flung the gemstones into different piles, counting as they went. Rubies made the smallest pile, then emeralds, then diamonds and sapphires. The pile of pearls was by far the biggest.

"Let's see if we're right." Teggs put a ruby in hole one, an emerald in hole two, a diamond in hole three, a sapphire in hole four and – finally – a pearl in hole five.

A strange light seemed to shimmer through the stones . . .

And suddenly the pyramid's door slid smoothly open!

"Result!" Tute jumped for joy, almost losing his headdress. "I don't know who those bandaged buffoons were, but I'd like to thank them for showing us the way inside!"

"Yes, they were running on the spot on top of it, weren't they?" Staring into the thick darkness beyond the door, Arx's smile faded. "But how could T. rex builders have come up with such a clever way to open the door?"

"Perhaps someone helped them," said Teggs.

"But who?" Tute gazed around, looking spooked.

"Come on," said Teggs grimly. "I think we should explore. Carefully!"

Slowly, ready for anything, the three dinosaurs entered the mysterious pyramid . . .

Iggy and Gipsy zoomed over the empty desert, pushing Tute's space-car to the limit as they raced back to the resort.

"Turn left at the next sand dune, Ig," said Gipsy, her nose in a map. "You know, I still can't believe we found T. rexes at that pyramid."

36

"If you found that hard to believe, how are you going to feel about *this*?" Iggy pointed through the windscreen. "Look!"

A battered spaceship was dropping down into sight ahead of them. It looked like an enormous flying saucer with a dark glass dome on top and huge metal claws emerging from its base. Crimson skulls with jagged teeth had been stencilled on the spaceship's side ...

Gipsy gasped. "Iggy, that's a carnivore ship!"

"A Dung-Puncher War-Craft Three Thousand, to be precise," said Iggy, who could spot all kinds of spaceship a mile off. "Designed and built by T. rexes – and most likely steered by them too."

Suddenly two bolts of sizzling energy spat from the spaceship.

"They're attacking us!" Gipsy yelled as Iggy swerved wildly to avoid the shots. "We've got nothing to fight back with – and we're still hours from the resort."

"We *must* reach Shuttle Alpha and warn the DSS," cried Iggy, watching another laser bolt scorch past. "An invasion like this could start a new Galaxy War."

Gipsy's head-crest flushed blue with alarm. "And it looks like we'll be its first casualties. If only we could contact the captain and warn him what's happening!"

"No communicators – this is supposed to be a holiday!" Iggy pushed the planet-rover's engines to the max, driving at over one hundred miles per hour – but the invading ship was way faster. "We can't outrun that thing. It'll blast us to bits at any moment!"

Gipsy and Iggy watched helplessly as the sinister spacecraft shot past them overhead. The metal claws around its base opened up like rusty petals, and a beam of brilliant light shone out – engulfing the space-car completely.

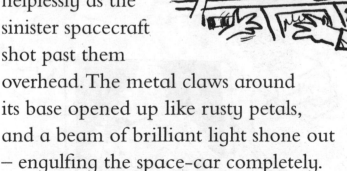

"We've lost all power," cried Iggy as the engines sputtered and died and the space-car started to rise up into the air. "And now we're being sucked inside!"

"That light . . ." Gipsy slumped against Iggy as the T. rex ship loomed larger and larger above them. "Making me dizzy."

"Me too," gasped Iggy. "Dizzy and sleepy . . ."

As the T. rex saucer swallowed them up, the lights switched off and left them in blackness . . .

Chapter Four

A T. REX TRAP

Back at the pyramid, Teggs, Tute and
Arx were exploring the cold, gloomy
chamber on the other side of the
pyramid door. Always prepared, Tute had
brought along a small torch. Its light
picked out stone pillars and archways
and spooky statues of weird, three-legged
creatures with oval heads.

"They'll be worth a fortune!" Tute
chuckled. "I bet this whole place is
stuffed full of loot."

"Where?" wondered Teggs. "I can't see
any other rooms or doors."

"They must be hidden." Tute shuffled
round in a circle, training his torch beam

carefully
all about.
A large
mosaic
covered
much of
the wall
in front of
them. It was
divided into
sixteen
squares,
and inside
every square
was a different
pattern of circles and dots.

"What an amazing design!" Arx
declared. "It reminds me of something."

Tute stared, puzzled. "Well, it certainly
doesn't remind me of T. rexes. They
mostly draw rude pictures of poos and
big bottoms." He pointed to one of the
statues. "As for this, it's way too delicate

for tyrannosaurs – their sculptures are big, lumpy things, carved with their claws. I've never seen anything like this stuff before."

"The mummy T rexes said it was their pyramid." Arx pondered. "But perhaps they didn't build it. Perhaps they only found it."

"Like we've found it now," Teggs agreed. "Pyramids and mummies were first invented by ancient Egyptosauruses – weren't they?"

Tute shrugged. "Some history experts believe we copied the idea from aliens we met in space thousands of years ago, during the long journey from Earth. But *our* pyramids were just triangular houses. And our mummies didn't move about – they were dead as doornails and stayed that way."

Teggs shuddered at the thought of the sinister mummies. Just where had they gone?

"Hey!" Arx cried, making Teggs and Tute jump. "I know what these pictures remind me of – star charts!" He pointed to dots and lines inside the first square. "That looks like the Pibble Nebula that marks the start of the Jurassic Quadrant, see? And this one over here looks like the Great Moonfield Reef in the Vegmeat Zone."

"You're right!" Teggs peered more closely. "That square there could easily show Raptos and its surrounding planets. And the pattern in the last one reminds me of the view of deep space we saw from Outpost Q . . ."

"So it's not just a pretty pattern," Tute murmured. "It's a journey through the galaxy."

"Exactly! Starting here in square three, travelling through here, here, here and here . . ." As he talked, Teggs tapped his tail against the patterns. ". . . And finally ending up in square four!"

And with a heavy, grinding sound, the stone wall split in half – and slid open to reveal an even bigger room beyond!

Tute punched the air in excitement. "Teggsy, you rock! You opened the hidden door! Come on, let's go."

"Wait." Arx was looking worried. "Square two shows a part of space that has only been discovered by dinosaurs in the last few years. That means that this place *must* have been built by aliens."

"Aliens who knew about the Jurassic Quadrant long before we did." Teggs nodded. "But *why* did they build this pyramid? What happened to them? And where did all those T. rexes vanish to, one thousand years ago?"

Tute shone his torch into the next chamber – and gulped. "Er, Teggsy? I'd say some of them ended up right here."

A tingle of fear shivered down Teggs's spine, and Arx gasped. The entire floor was littered with little arm-bones, giant leg bones and massive skulls with teeth like spikes.

"A room full of T. rex skeletons," Teggs whispered. "Something terrible must've happened here . . . but what?"

"Never mind that." Tute pointed to something sparkling beyond the bones. "More jewels. Brilliant!" Eagerly, he rushed inside.

"Careful, Tute!" Teggs and Arx started after him.

And as soon as they were all inside – GRRRR-THUNK! The wall slid closed again.

"Hey!" Teggs spun round and banged on the stone with his tail. But the wall would not open again. "We're trapped!"

"Sorry, fellas," said Tute, scooping up the jewels. "When I saw these, I ran in here without thinking."

Suddenly a grating, scraping noise sounded above their heads. A triangular hole was opening in the stone ceiling.

"There's another door!" said Tute brightly.

"So there is," said
Teggs. "But we don't
know if it's a way out
for us – or a way in for
something else ..."

As if in answer, a large
metal figure floated
down through the hole
in the roof. It had three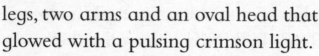
legs, two arms and an oval head that
glowed with a pulsing crimson light.

"Hide!" Teggs hissed as he and Arx
ducked behind the nearest skeleton.

Tute scurried after them. "What IS that
thing?"

"It looks like a robot," Arx murmured.
"It's the same shape as the statues we
saw in the entrance hall."

Slowly, the robot turned its head
towards them – and a ray of red light
shot out at the skeleton!

"Look out!" Teggs rolled over
backwards, pushing his friends clear as

the bones exploded in flames. "That thing's got a death ray – and it's not afraid to use it!"

Tute joined the astrosaurs as they scrambled for shelter behind another pile of bones. "Now we know why there are so many skeletons in here."

But as the robot slowly bobbed towards their hollow hiding place, another secret doorway opened in the wall behind it.

"Right," Teggs breathed. "Arx, Tute – I'll distract old rust-head here, you make a dash for that door. Don't argue – just go!"

So saying, he sprang out of hiding and performed a spiky somersault. ZAPP! The robot fired its deadly ray at Teggs, missing him by millimetres. A stone pillar shook and smoked under the attack.

"Now!" Arx commanded, sprinting for the door with Tute.

But before they could reach the open door – "OWW!" The two dinosaurs shook, surrounded by sparks. It was as if they had run into an invisible electric cushion.

"What happened?" Teggs yelled, ducking as the robot fired again and another pile of bones went up in flames. "Why can't you get out?"

"The door is protected by an energy screen!" Arx groaned. "An invisible barrier we can't get through."

"Watch out!" called Teggs as the robot turned and sped towards Arx and Tute, its head glowing redder and redder, ready to fire. "From this distance, it can't miss!"

Chapter Five

THE TEST AND THE TERROR

Just as the robot was about to fire, Teggs threw a humungous hip-bone at its back and spoiled its aim. ZZAP! The floor at Tute's feet burst into flames.

"Whoa!" Tute jumped aside and banged his head on a pillar. As Arx dashed to help him up, he noticed a bank of buttons and switches set into the stone. "Hey! These look like the controls for the energy screen!"

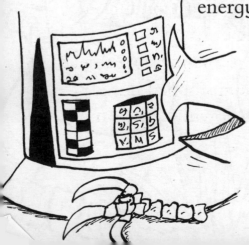

"Can you work them, Arx?" called Teggs.

"I'm not sure," said Arx. "The

system is alien."

"You've *got* to do it!" Tute urged him, scurrying away to join Teggs. "We'll try to keep laser-face off your back!"

The floating robot spun round to face Teggs and Tute and fired again. Teggs threw himself to the floor but the deadly ray came so close that his backplates were almost burned black. Tute ran in the opposite direction, drawing the robot's fire.

"I think I've worked it out!" Arx carefully tapped the buttons and flicked the switches. "Try now."

Tute sprinted over to the invisible shield – and this time nothing stopped him. "The energy screen's down! Come on, you guys – scram!"

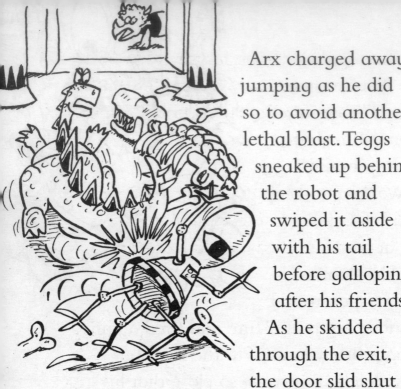

Arx charged away, jumping as he did so to avoid another lethal blast. Teggs sneaked up behind the robot and swiped it aside with his tail before galloping after his friends. As he skidded through the exit, the door slid shut behind him. Arx helped Teggs up, and together they listened at the door for any signs that the robot was coming after them.

But the room remained silent.

"Well done, Arx," said Teggs gratefully.

Arx puffed out a breath. "I'm starting to think that if this pyramid really does belong to those T. rex mummies, they're welcome to it!"

Tute quickly shone his torch about to reveal a long narrow corridor that stretched on into pitch darkness. "One thing I don't get, guys," he panted. "If that robot's job is to kill intruders, why not attack us straight away? Why wait till we'd entered an empty room?"

"And why block the exit with an energy screen, but leave the controls that switch it off in plain sight?" Arx pondered. "It's almost like we're being tested."

"You could be right." Tute looked around nervously in the darkness. "The jewel code to open the pyramid door was an intelligence test . . . the star-charts mosaic tested our knowledge of space travel . . ."

"And luckily Arx has just passed the 'switching off an alien energy screen' test," Teggs concluded. "I think that this pyramid was built for a very important reason – and if we can only survive these tests, perhaps we'll find out what it is!"

Unaware of the danger their friends had been facing, Iggy and Gipsy woke in a daze.

"Ig, where are we?" groaned Gipsy. She was tied up beside him, lying on a filthy metal floor. "What happened to Tute's car?"

"We were dragged into the T. rex spaceship, remember?"

Iggy banged his bound feet against thick metal bars. "They must have dumped us in their cells."

Gipsy saw the bloodstains on the wall and shivered. "At least they didn't eat us."

"Not yet," came a gruff, biting voice. "Us must question you first!"

The two astrosaurs twisted round and found an enormous, drooling T. rex in battered space-armour on the other side of the bars. "Allow myself to introduce me – Brigadier Skunch, most feared and hated T. rex warlord in universe."

"Never heard of you." Iggy sniffed and spluttered. "But you didn't mention you're also the whiffiest!"

"Oh, yes! Thank you, me forgot."
Skunch sniffed his armpits with pride.
"Now. To business. Us have already
melted down your car for scrap. But
for you, us have something nastier in
mind . . ." He pulled a chunky red gun
from his hip holster and aimed it at Iggy.
"This is my roast-rifle."

"Is it?" Although Gipsy was scared
of the huge, drooling brigadier, she
was determined not to show it. "How
interesting."

"See, you is not just my prisoners
– you is my evening meal! So while me
questions you, me can cook you too."
Skunch narrowed his eyes. "What have
you found in the pyramid down there?"

Iggy winked at Gipsy. "Er . . . what
pyramid?"

"Us KNOW you know about
pyramid," Skunch roared. "Us KNOW
that you is astrosaurs, here to guard it."
PZZZZZT! He opened fire.

"Aargh!" Iggy yelped as his whole body glowed red and started to sizzle. "I'm . . . burning . . ."

"Leave him alone!" Gipsy snapped. "If you cook us you'll never get the answers you need."

Skunch switched off the rifle. "Lucky for you me also like my food raw," he hissed.

Iggy lay gasping in a sweaty heap. "How . . . did you know . . . we were astrosaurs?"

"Us have spy machines," Skunch

gloated. "Us read Tute the treasure-
hunter's space-mail to Captain Teggs
Stegosaur – 'Come quick, me found
T. rex pyramid.'" He narrowed his eyes
and growled. "So, now you knows that
me knows you knows about pyramid, tell
me what you knows or I will EAT your
nose – knows what I mean?"

"Nose," said Iggy. "I mean, *No*!
We don't know anything about the
pyramid."

Skunch aimed his roast-rifle again.

"It's true!" cried Gipsy. "You should know that two T. rexes turned up and attacked us before we could get inside."

"WHAT?" Skunch bellowed. "What is you on about?"

"Those two T. rexes covered in bandages," said Iggy. "I suppose it was their idea of a good disguise for hanging out near a pyramid."

"You is a liar," growled Skunch. "Me not send anyone. Me just arrived."

Gipsy looked at Iggy in alarm. "Then if Skunch didn't send those T. rexes we met . . . they must've been *real* mummies!"

"You be needing your mummy to cry to," sneered Skunch, "once my three ships full of extra-angry, super-violent troops start attacking this puny planet."

Iggy gulped.
"All because of the
pyramid?"
Skunch nodded.
"Pyramid retreat here
was biggest ever T. rex defeat.
Pyramid BAD place. One thousand
years ago, great Lord Ganster found it
there in the sand. He passed BAD tests
to get inside – but something BAD was
waiting. It turned Ganster BAD too. He
tricked hundreds of T. rexes into rushing
inside BAD pyramid – where something
BAD happened to them. BAD, BAAAAD,
BAAAAAAAAAAAD!"

"That's too bad," said Iggy.

"Us . . . ran away." Skunch shuddered.
"But all these years later, us tougher and
even meaner and not scared of dumb
curses." He stamped so hard on the floor
he left a dent in it. "So – to save the
glory of the T. rex race, now pyramid has
been found, us will SMASH it to bits!"

Suddenly – BEEP! – Brigadier Skunch's communicator, tied tightly around his little arm, lit up.

"Me got message from troops," he growled, and held the device to his ear.

"Ig," Gipsy hissed. "We left the captain, Arx and Tute trying to get inside the pyramid. They'll be defenceless when Skunch and his troops attack."

Iggy nodded worriedly. "We've got to do something!"

"You WILL do something, you plant-eating plonk-heads." Skunch swung

63

back round to face them. "You and your friends will fill stomachs at T. rex victory feast!"

Gipsy swallowed hard. "Pardon?"

"My troops has been spying on pyramid. They told me your friends has gone inside and not come out again. So, if the BAD something is still there, it will be busy with your friends while us launch surprise attack." Skunch laughed heartily. "And fighting makes us hungry – so when us finish, us shall eat all plant-eaters on holiday here!"

Iggy and Gipsy swapped horrified looks.

"Guards," Skunch bellowed, "take these plant-eating ploppers to the kitchens." He licked his lips and leered at the two astrosaurs. "Us shall be winners – and you shall be DINNERS!"

Chapter Six

CHILLING CHALLENGES

Inside the pyramid, Teggs, Arx and Tute
were walking carefully through the dark,
narrow corridor.

"I just noticed,"
said Tute, looking
at his wrist.
"My watch has
stopped. It's still
showing the time
it was when we first
went inside this place."

"I wonder how long
we've been here," said
Teggs. "The funny thing is, I'm not at all
hungry. That just *never* happens."

"I've lost my appetite too." Arx pointed a few metres ahead of them. "But we've found the end of the passage."

Tute peered into the gloom and saw another door cut into the stone.

As they approached, it slid slowly open.

"What's waiting for us this time?" Arx wondered.

As if to answer his question, the room was suddenly flooded with light from a crystal chandelier hanging down from the high ceiling. The room was bigger than the others. Lining its great walls were giant vases, exotic sculptures and beautiful tapestries. But taking Teggs's attention in the centre of the room was something large and lumpy, hidden beneath a white sheet.

"What's that?" Arx whispered. "Another robot?"

"There's only one way to find out." Teggs led the way slowly into the room, and hooked one of his tail spikes onto

the edge of the white sheet. WHOOSH!
He snatched the fabric away . . .

To reveal coils of cable and a mini-
mountain of mechanical parts.

Tute scratched his head. "What's that
lot doing here?"

Suddenly the door scraped shut

behind them, sealing them inside – and a deep, harsh voice boomed all around them. "This entire room is a bomb," the voice announced. "To prevent a deadly explosion, you must construct a working spacecraft engine from the spare parts in front of you before the lights go out. If you fail, you will die. If you succeed, you will get the reward you deserve. Your time starts . . . now!"

"Wait!" Teggs shouted. "Who are you? Where are you? Why have you set all these tests?"

But the voice remained silent as the lights in the chandelier began to flash. One of the crystals quickly turned dark.

Tute gulped. "I count ninety-nine crystals still lit."

"Make that ninety-eight," said Teggs grimly as another went out. "Arx, what do you think – can we build an engine in time?"

"If Iggy was here, no problem." Arx

looked
worried.
"But a lot
of these
parts are
alien – I'm
not sure
what they
do."

"You can be
sure what this
room will do if
we *can't* pass
this test,"
said Tute,
looking at
the flashing
lights.

"It'll go
BOOOM!"
On board the T. rex
spaceship, still tied up, Gipsy and Iggy

were being
carried to
the kitchens
by two of
Skunch's
guards. The
deeper down into the ship they went,
the worse the smell of boiled blood and
barbecued blubber became.

Finally they were dropped on a greasy
floor. "There," grunted one of the T. rexes.
"Now us must get ready for BATTLE."

Chuckling as if this were the funniest
thing either of them had heard, the two
carnivores stomped away.

"Ugh!" groaned Gipsy. "This can't be
the kitchen."

"It's more like a toilet," Iggy agreed.
Piles of vile-smelling slop sat steaming
in buckets. A rusting pile of pots and
pans lay in the enormous sink. Dirty
plates littered the floor, and cockroaches
scuttled all about them. Suddenly the

floor lurched beneath them.

"Brigadier Skunch must be heading towards the pyramid," Gipsy realized. "And Teggs, Arx and Tute are still inside it!"

"And where are we when they need us?" Iggy sighed. "Trussed up in the nastiest kitchen in space."

"There is old T. rex saying," growled a super-fat T. rex with one eye, one arm and a wooden leg as he hobbled inside, a dirty chef's hat perched on his head. "'The muckier the kitchen, the better the food!'" The newcomer laughed nastily. "And in a kitchen as mucky as mine, you will taste DEE-lish!"

Gipsy struggled up. "Who are you?"

"Me is Chef Sheff – Brigadier Skunch's personal cook." He pointed out his missing

body-parts with his good claw. "Me can't fight so well, so me cooks instead."

"Right." Iggy turned up his nose. "I suppose you lost those body bits in space battles?"

"Nope. Me use them as ingredients in special pie. Though me say so myself, me v tasty T. rex!" Chef Sheff smiled. "And me bets that YOU is scrummy too. Me thinks me will cook you with dung jelly. Where be my roast-rifle?" He rummaged through a rusty kitchen drawer and finally unearthed the rifle. "Aha! Now me can cook you . . ."

"Guess again, meat-mush," growled Gipsy. "Because the guards who brought us here didn't notice me cutting my ropes on their claws. And now I've wriggled FREE!" She jumped in the air, performed a graceful somersault, and kicked Chef Sheff right in the belly. He doubled up and collapsed in a heap. She grabbed the roast-rifle, quickly crossed to

Iggy and fired at the ropes that held his wrists and ankles fast.

"Way to go, Gipsy!" Iggy struggled up and hugged her. "Now we've got to get out of here and warn Captain Teggs."

"How?" Gipsy looked around helplessly. "We may be loose, but we're still stuck on this spaceship."

"Maybe not." Iggy grabbed the roast-rifle, set it to the highest level, and pointed it at the kitchen floor. Very soon, the scuffed metal began to bubble and blur into a smoky, molten mess. "We're on the lowest level of the ship, right?"

Gipsy shrugged. "So?"

"So, here you go . . ." Suddenly a hot wind blew up at them, clearing the smoke – to reveal a large hole had been burned through the bottom of the spaceship. "Ta-daa! Instant escape route. When the saucer lands, we jump out and race into that pyramid ahead of Skunch's poop-heads."

"But even if we can warn the captain and Arx, what happens then?" Gipsy's face fell. "With a T. rex army on our tails we'll be sniffed out in seconds. We won't stand a chance!"

Chapter Seven

WIN OR LOSE?

At that moment, deep inside the pyramid, Teggs knew that his own chances of survival were shrinking all the time.

He, Arx and Tute were covered in oil and sweat, struggling to turn the pile of mechanical parts into a working spacecraft engine. Several times Teggs thought they'd cracked it – but still the engine stubbornly refused to start. The room was getting steadily darker as the crystals on the chandelier went out one by one.

Angrily, Teggs shouted out at the mysterious voice. "Why are you making us do this? We don't mean you any harm!"

"It's no good," groaned Tute. "This whole room's going to explode at any moment."

"Tute, try sticking those red cables into the booster jets," Arx suggested. "Captain, let's reverse the exhaust section and *then* plug it into the ignition circuit."

"It's about the only thing we haven't tried!" Teggs agreed.

Grunting with effort, straining to see in the gloom, the dinosaurs shifted the heavy metal components and plugged in the final wires.

"Only ten lights left!" Tute whispered, wiping his brow. "Start her up, Teggsy!"

"Horns crossed!" said Arx as Teggs pressed the big red button . . .

And nothing happened.

Arx groaned. "That's it, then."

"No! It's got to be right." Teggs started hammering the button with his tail. "Come on, work!" he snarled, whacking it harder and harder. "*Work!*"

Finally, with a throaty, warbling growl, the engine started.

"Yesssss!" Tute ran around the room with his arms in the air as if he'd just scored a winning goal, and Teggs whooped as brilliant blue flames poured from the booster jets.

"You have passed the test." The voice boomed out, making them jump. "But that is bad luck for you."

"Eh?" Tute scowled as the booster rockets died. "What do you mean?"

"This pyramid is a computer-controlled prison," the voice revealed. "By breaking inside and passing these tests you have been judged greedy enough, clever enough and skilled enough to release Keprish."

"Who's Keprish?" Teggs wondered. "Who are YOU?"

But the voice grew louder, drowning him out. "Hear us, Keprish! We imprisoned you here for crimes against the universe, never to be released. Did you truly believe we would allow ANYONE to set you free? No, Keprish. We have teased you with false hope . . . allowed you to imagine that, perhaps this time, you might actually escape. HA! Watch and suffer as your would-be rescuers DIE!"

"What are you on about?" Teggs shouted. "We didn't come here to rescue anyone!"

But then the dinosaurs gasped as ten glowing robots — each identical to the one they'd fought in the force-field chamber — dropped down from the ceiling, their blank faces pulsing with deadly power. With incredible speed they formed a tight circle around Teggs, Arx and Tute. Teggs clobbered one with his tail, but the blow had no effect. Arx tried to charge at the robots, but he was knocked straight back again.

"Begin the execution!" hissed the voice from nowhere. "These fools had the power to set you free, Keprish. Now they will be destroyed!"

As the robots' faces grew blindingly bright, Teggs looked around wildly for any hope of escape – and was startled to find a bandaged T. rex burst out from beneath a tapestry on the opposite wall! Another came out behind it, and then two more ... *three* more ...

"Look out," he cried. "Mummies!"

"Oh, great!" Tute closed his eyes as *twelve* of the mummified monsters charged towards them. "Now there's a queue to kill us!"

But to Teggs's amazement, the mummies attacked the robots! The assault took some of the machines by surprise. Sparks blew out of the back of their heads, and they clattered to

the ground. But the other robots spun round and blasted the T. rexes. Four were dissolved to dust, but the others kept on attacking, biting and slashing and stomping on their mechanical foes.

"T. rexes on our side?" Arx looked baffled. "Since when?"

"Don't knock it, Arx," said Teggs, dodging a face-blast. "We need all the help we can get." With a mighty swish of his tail he whapped the nearest robot round the back of the head – cracking it open like a crystal egg. "Hit them from behind," he yelled. "That's their weak spot!"

Arx got stuck in straight away, knocking over two robots and trampling them into the ground. Tute whacked one robot in the back with his bag of jewels, sending it straight into the path of three mummies, who fell upon it, snapping their jaws hungrily. *ZZAPP!* The remaining robots destroyed the carnivores – but while they were distracted, Teggs and Arx attacked from the rear, using tail and horn to devastating effect. Both robots went up in smoke . . .

"It's over," Teggs realized. All that was left of the glowing robots was a mess of cracked-open cases and electronic innards. And all but one of the T. rex mummies had been turned to dust. The sole survivor stood still as a statue, his eyes blank.

"That mummy's friends gave their lives to save us," Arx said quietly.

"Them . . . my servants," came a deep growl behind them.

Teggs and his friends turned to find a huge, powerful figure stepping through a secret door behind the tapestry. It was another T. rex – only this one was bandage-free. Like Tute, he was dressed in fine, flowing robes and a striped headband with a jewel in its centre. But it was his eyes that stood out the most – cold and glassy and colourless.

"Who are you?" Teggs demanded, tail raised and ready to fight.

The T. rex didn't seem to hear him. "Us blundered through most tests, but could not build the engine. Bomb went off. My servants shielded me, but got hurt from head to foot."

"Then . . . *that's* why they wore bandages?" Arx stared at the mummy in wonder. "To help their injuries?"

Teggs frowned. "Why help us now? They fought us outside."

"Them was not attacking you. Them went out to uncover the entrance key so you could get inside." The T. rex nodded slowly. "Now there be only one left. But after one thousand years of service . . . me was bored of them anyway!"

"Is that all you can say?" Teggs began angrily.

"Wait a sec, Teggsy. I recognize that face . . ." Tute was suddenly looking very scared. "I don't believe it. That T. rex looks exactly like Lord Ganster – the one who discovered the pyramid, a thousand years ago!"

Chapter Eight

DEEPER TROUBLE

"We're very near the pyramid now, Gipsy." On board Brigadier Skunch's spaceship, Iggy was peering out through the hole he'd made in the kitchen floor. "I think we're coming in to land!"

"Then get ready to jump." Gipsy came over holding a big bundle of bloodstained tablecloths. "I found these in a kitchen drawer and knotted them together – we can use them as a kind of parachute and get out ahead of the T. rexes."

"Good thinking." Iggy grinned at her. "The more time we have to reach the captain, Arx and Tute, the better."

Now Gipsy could see the pyramid through the hole too, like a giant spearhead sticking through the sand. "Well, no time like the present, I suppose." With a tum full of butterflies, she took one side of the tablecloths. Iggy tucked the roast-rifle under his arm and gripped the other side.

"Three, two, one — *skydive!*" Iggy closed his eyes and jumped through the hole.

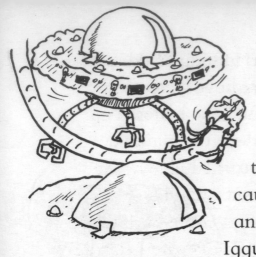

Gipsy followed a
split second later.
"Whooooosh!"
she yelled as
the sandy wind
caught the fabric
and sent her and
Iggy tumbling
through the air. The yellow sand and
blue sky blurred together as the two
astrosaurs spun in wide circles past the
three T. rex warcraft, drifting down faster
and faster . . .

"OOOF!" Iggy and Gipsy landed
clumsily on top of a sand dune and
rolled all the way down it, finally
slithering to a stop at the base of the
pyramid.

"We did it!" Gipsy
spat sand from
her mouth. "We
survived the drop
bang on target!"

"But look," groaned Iggy. "I don't know how the captain got into the pyramid, but the entrance is closed up again!"

Gipsy's headcrest turned blue as she saw that he was right – and bluer still as the T. rex spaceships came in to land in a roaring rush of smoke, their clawed undersides digging into the sand. "But if we can't get in, there's nothing we can do!"

"Wait! Remember those bandaged T. rexes we ran into? They appeared from nowhere and vanished again." Iggy scrambled up. "Tute said there could be a secret way into the pyramid. We'd better get looking and hope we find it fast."

"No, you don't. Come back here!" The chubby figure of Chef Sheff squeezed out through the hole they had made in the kitchen. "Brigadier Skunch, quick! Our evening meal's making a run for it!"

"Uh-oh," said Iggy, helping Gipsy to her hooves. "Time we weren't here." Then Skunch himself dropped down through the hole, looking meatier and mightier than ever in his full T. rex battle-armour. Growling angrily, he pulled out a pistol and fired laser beams at Iggy and Gipsy. They dashed for the shelter of the pyramid.

"Me can't be doing with this," Skunch rumbled. "Me got invasion to lead. But you'd better catch the plant-eaters, Sheff — or us be chewing on you before the day is through!"

Panting for breath, pressed up against the side of the pyramid, Gipsy gave Iggy a hopeful smile. "At least it won't be too hard to outrun a fat, one-legged meatchomper in all this sand."

But then they heard Sheff hollering through the hole in the bottom of the ship: "Kitchen hands, get down here and carry me. NOW!"

Three colossal, overweight T. rexes in filthy white overalls came scrambling out, snarling and snapping like crocodiles.

"Run for it, Gipsy," Iggy cried. "If we can't find a hidden way into this pyramid – we're dead!"

* * *

Back in the chamber of the bomb, Teggs was wide-eyed and Arx's horns were curling with shock at the sight of the menacing T. rex.

Tute was all a-tremble. "This is the craziest treasure hunt I've ever been on, Teggsy," he whispered. "I'm not sure I can take much more!"

"Hang in there, Tute," whispered Teggs. "I think we're close to getting some real answers around here."

He raised his voice and turned to the T. rex. "Well? Are you the same Lord Ganster – one thousand years later?"

The cold-eyed T. rex nodded. "Pyramid sealed with special barrier that holds back time." The hissed words came haltingly, as if spoken with a great effort. "Nothing grows old here. No need for food or water."

"So that's why we've lost our appetites," Teggs realized.

Tute nodded. "And why my watch stopped working."

"And why such an old pyramid still looks like new," Arx concluded. "A time-resistant force field – amazing technology!"

"Scarabs is smartest beings in universe." Ganster paused, then raised an arm stiffly and lifted the tapestry with one claw. "Keprish wants to see you."

The mummy T. rex jerked into life, stomping towards the dinosaurs. "See you, NOW."

Tute gulped. "I don't want to see him!"

"Quick, pretend to faint," Teggs

whispered. "Ganster sent his mummies outside so there must be a hidden exit around here. When we've gone, try to find it – in case we need to make a quick getaway!"

"Gotcha." Tute winked at Teggs. Then he pretended to swoon and fell to the floor.

"Our friend is unwell," Teggs told Ganster.

"Leave him," snarled the T. rex as the mummy bundled Teggs and Arx towards the tapestry. "You two most important to Keprish."

The two astrosaurs soon found themselves shoved into Keprish's lair. It was cavernous and grand and piled high with gold and jewels and big dusty treasure chests. The ceiling was lost from sight in shadow, but Teggs guessed it stretched right up to the pyramid's pointed roof. A massive emerald as big as a table was fixed to one wall. Big TV screens showing views of the pyramid's rooms lined another.

A white, pyramid-shaped rocket stood in one cobwebby corner. But Ganster crossed straight to a great stone altar in the middle of the room, where an alien figure lay. It was ancient, oval-headed with three spindly legs and a single closed eye, dressed in robes and a headdress like Ganster and Tute.

"Here is great Keprish," said Ganster.

"So that's what a Scarab looks like," Arx murmured. "The robots and statues we saw are based on them."

Suddenly, both Ganster and the bandaged T. rex jerked and slumped, as if they were just empty suits of skin. And the eye of the creature on the altar snapped open, bright and purple, making Teggs and Arx jump.

"At last," Keprish hissed, through a mean little mouth in the centre of its eyeball. "After thousands of years, you have come . . . the creatures who shall set me free!"

Chapter Nine

THE POWER OF KEPRISH

"Er . . . Hi, Keprish!" Teggs forced a smile.
"If we'd known you were here, we'd have
brought grapes."

"You're dressed like our friend lying
down outside," Arx told Keprish. "Did
you used to live on Egyptus?"

"Yes. We ruled this entire sector of
space," Keprish replied. "Lesser beings
we encountered worshipped us as gods,
and copied our clothes and
customs."

"Dinosaurs aren't
'lesser beings'," Teggs
said sharply. "Tute was
the one who found this

pyramid in the first place."

"Many have found it, these last ten thousand years," hissed Keprish. "Trapped for all time behind an energy screen, unable to move, I have watched them take the tests on these screens — and watched them fail."

"That strikes me as odd." Teggs tapped the air above Keprish — and snatched his hand away as blue crackles stung his skin. "I mean, this is a prison. Why do the Scarabs want to tempt others inside? And why set them tests instead of just killing them?"

"You heard the voice of my jailers," snarled Keprish. "They have seen fit to torture me by leaving the tiniest hope that some day I might get free." He narrowed his eye. "Why do you think they left my mind free but my body rooted to the spot? Why do you think they left all my wealth in here with me, knowing I could never spend it? Why do you think they left me my rocket ship, knowing I could never repair its ruined engines?"

Teggs frowned. "You must have done a lot of bad things to make them want to treat you so meanly. Just what were you locked up for, Keprish?"

"Hardly anything!" Keprish scowled. "All I did was rob eight hundred space-banks, blow up twenty-two worlds, exterminate fifteen alien races and do a wee in the Scarab Queen's bathtub!"

Arx swapped a very worried look with Teggs. "Er . . . is that all?"

"And so now, this computerized prison is programmed to lure other races inside." Keprish dribbled and hissed with rage. "It spits out my jewels to tempt in the unwary. Then the computer tries to taunt me by forcing you to demonstrate your skills. When you passed the star-chart test, you showed your knowledge of space. So if I made you my crew, you could take me anywhere in the universe . . ."

"And we proved we can break through energy screens like the one that holds you, *and* that we can repair spaceship engines too."

"But someone must've broken through the pyramid's shield already," said Teggs. "Ganster sent his servants out to find us. Didn't you?"

Ganster still stood with his head slumped beside his motionless mummy.

"The shield is *not* broken. One brick in the pyramid is loose, to let in air, that is all." Keprish sighed crossly. "My puppets can get out – but trapped by this energy screen, I cannot."

Teggs was puzzled. "Your puppets?"

"That's right." Keprish smiled slyly. "I control Ganster and his followers. Observe . . ."

Suddenly Ganster and the mummy started hopping on the spot. Then the mummy did a handstand while Ganster started smacking his own bottom.

"These poor fools have been my puppets for a thousand years," Keprish went on. "Thanks to that brain-stone on the wall behind you."

Teggs turned and saw the enormous emerald on the wall. "What's a brain-stone?"

Keprish smiled. "The Scarabs made one big mistake when they buried me here with my possessions – they thought that the brain-stone was just a giant jewel." He chuckled. "In fact, it magnifies the power of my mind. Anyone who touches it is mine to command! Once I had taken control of Ganster and his slaves, I made him summon hundreds more T. rexes to the pyramid and trapped them inside."

"What happened to them then?" Teggs demanded.

"Me show you," growled Ganster,

jerking back into life under Keprish's control. The carnivore crossed to a plush velvet curtain and ripped it aside to reveal a hidden room . . .

A room stuffed from floor to ceiling with sleeping T. rexes!

"Behold," Keprish purred proudly. "My hidden army of unquestioning carnivores that will one day conquer the galaxy!"

Gipsy and Iggy hared across the sand, laser bolts whizzing past their heads. The two T. rex kitchen helpers were carrying Chef Sheff on their shoulders, and he was firing wildly at his escaping dinners.

"Not matter to me if me has to char-grill you with laser instead of roasting you!" he yelled. "Me just season you with extra dung pepper!"

"Remind me to look up the recipe," joked Iggy. He tried to turn and fire the roast-rifle, but Sheff kept shooting and he had to dodge and duck.

"How are we ever going to find a hidden way into the pyramid while we're dodging those meat-gobblers . . ." Gipsy trailed off, then skidded to a stop, pointing halfway up the pyramid wall. "Look!"

With amazement, Iggy spotted a scrap of bandage flapping from between two

 enormous bricks like a grubby flag. "You think one of the mummies tore that while squeezing through a secret gap in the brickwork?"

"I think it's
worth checking
out!" Gipsy ran
up to the
pyramid
and started
climbing
the steep wall,
gripping onto
every crack
and crevice
as hard as she could.
Iggy came scaling the sheer surface
behind her, feet slipping, claws scraping
the stone, desperate not to fall.

But Chef Sheff and his friends were
quickly catching up. Just as the two
astrosaurs reached the fluttering bandage,
the T. rexes gathered beneath them.

Gipsy tugged on the giant brick with
all her strength. "It won't budge!"

"It's got to," gasped Iggy, heaving and
straining to shift it. "It must!"

"Prepare to be cooked, plant-scoffers!"
yelled Chef Sheff. While his kitchen boys
jeered and dribbled beside him, he took
careful aim . . .

Suddenly the heavy brick shot out of
the pyramid wall like the cash tray in a
supermarket till, barely missing the two
astrosaurs. It tumbled down the side
of the pyramid and smashed all
three T. rexes into the sand!

Iggy stared in
amazement. "How did
that happen?"

"I pushed it out from the inside! Easy."
Tute's head appeared through the hole in

the wall. "Wow, am I ever pleased to see you two."

Iggy grinned. "Where'd you spring from?"

"Things are mega-freaky-spooky in this place," Tute explained. "Teggsy sent me off to find the emergency exit."

"Right now, it's an emergency *entrance*." Gipsy clambered inside. "We must warn the captain and Arx – any minute now, three T. rex battle squads will be banging on the pyramid's doors."

Tute's face fell. "I don't believe it! *More* T. rexes?"

"What do you mean, *more*?" asked Iggy. "What's been going on?"

"If you're feeling brave enough," said Tute, "come in and find out!"

Chapter Ten

MENACE IN MIND

"I don't believe it," breathed Teggs. In Keprish's lair he was staring at the squashed-up sleeping T. rexes. "They're all still alive after so many centuries."

"Alive and in prime condition," said Keprish proudly. "The T. rex creatures are the most savage fighters I have ever encountered . . ." Suddenly he laughed. "And look! Just look at the screen! What incredible luck – here come some more!"

Teggs and Arx gasped to see a hundred bloodthirsty T. rex shock troops massing at the entrance to the pyramid.

"Hear me, Bad Something in pyramid!" bellowed their leader. "Me, Brigadier Skunch, will smash you for great T. rex defeat one thousand years ago. Doors not keep us out! Us know code 'cos was spying on the astrosaurs when they got in. Ruby, emerald, diamond, sapphire, pearl . . ."

The doors slid open, and Skunch led his rabble of 'rexes inside.

"A full-scale T. rex invasion?" Teggs gulped. "Well, at least they'll have to pass the pyramid's tests before they can get any further."

"No they won't," said Keprish. "It takes a whole day for the computer to re-set the tests."

Arx stared in horror as Skunch's troops tore into the star-system mosaics on the screen. "They'll use brute force to smash their way through – then they'll rip us apart!"

"Fear not, horned one," Keprish hissed. "I shall use Ganster to trick the T. rexes into touching the brain-stone. Then *my mind* shall invade the invaders and take control! I shall add these creatures to my army, ready to conquer whole worlds in the name of Keprish!" He smiled nastily at Teggs and Arx. "And now you're here to set me free, that conquest will soon

110

begin! The energy-screen controls are built into this altar. You must shut them down."

"No way!" Arx cried. "You're a monster."

"We'd sooner die than help you," Teggs added.

Keprish's big eye narrowed. "You have no choice. As soon as you touch the brain-stone, my mind will control yours."

"Then we *won't* touch it," said Teggs.

"Yes, you will," growled Ganster, grabbing hold of Teggs while his bandaged-up buddy seized Arx. Both T. rexes were incredibly strong. Neither astrosaur could break free.

"Look into the brain-stone," whispered Keprish as the massive emerald began

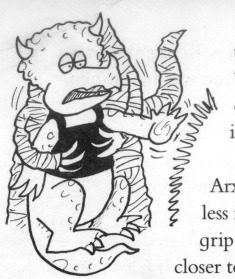

to sparkle.

"See its pretty colours . . . see how it shines . . ."

"It . . . it *does* shine." Arx began struggling less in the mummy's grip as it forced him closer to the evil jewel. "I want to touch it . . ."

"No, Arx!" Teggs struggled with all his might. "Do you want to end up like Ganster – a helpless puppet?" His head was throbbing. His vision was filled with the burning bright brain-stone.

"You WILL set me free!" cried Keprish. "Touch the stone! Let my mind control yours!"

"No!" gasped Teggs. Keprish's words echoed in his mind, drowning out all thoughts of resistance. His head was almost touching the brain-stone. Arx's horn was millimetres away.

"You cannot fight any longer!" laughed Keprish.

"Maybe they can't!" roared Iggy, bursting into the room with Gipsy and Tute. "But WE can!"

With a cry of "Hiiiiii-YAH!" Gipsy leaped through the air and kicked Ganster in the teeth. As the T. rex staggered backwards, Tute dived at Teggs in a rugby tackle, bringing him down.

Both dinosaurs fell against Arx, pushing
him away from the brain-stone.

"Who dares enter my domain?" raged
Keprish.

"Who else?" said Iggy.
"Astrosaurs!" He
lifted his stolen
roast-rifle and
aimed it at the
brain-stone.
"I don't know what
this thing is, but I'm
guessing it's nothing
cool. In fact, it looks
downright HOT!"
He blasted away

with the roast-rifle.
"Noooooooo!"
screamed Keprish as
the greenish stone
turned scarlet – and
then exploded into
a billion blazing

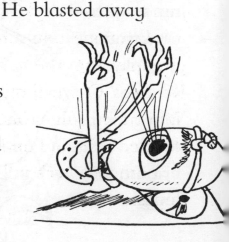

fragments.
The alien
shook as if
he'd been
electrocuted.
Then his eye
closed, and
his body was
still. Ganster roared

with pain and the mummy sank to his
knees. Finally, both T. rexes flopped over
backwards and lay still.

"Iggy! Gipsy! I'm so glad to see
you!" Teggs shook his aching head and
grinned. "We've been going out of our
minds with worry!"

"Well done, you three." Arx got up
groggily from the floor and looked at
Keprish. "Our evil alien's still breathing.
When the brain-stone blew up it must've
shocked his mind and knocked him out."

"Lord Ganster's still alive too," said
Teggs.

"Ganster?" echoed Gipsy and Iggy.

"Never mind all that, we've got to get out of here!" Tute scrambled to his feet and pointed to the screens. "Look!"

The pictures showed Skunch and his troops in the energy-screen room, firing

their powerful lasers at the door – which was starting to crumble.

"Once they get through that door there's only one more between them and the bomb chamber," Arx noted. "It won't take them long to sniff us out behind the tapestry!"

Teggs heard a chorus of low, growling yawns behind him, and frowned. "Uh-oh. As if all that wasn't enough, I think Keprish's sleeping

T. rex army next door is waking up."

"I guess Keprish's mind control was keeping them asleep," said Arx. "And when they wake up and see us, I don't think they'll be very friendly!"

Tute and Iggy stared boggle-eyed at the scaly, scrunched-up monsters as they snuffled and snorted. "This is a total nightmare!" wailed Gipsy.

"So what are we waiting for?" said Tute. "I found the secret exit – let's scram!"

"Scram where?" Gipsy shook her head. "We've lost your space-car, and Brigadier Skunch has got three T. rex warcraft parked outside. He's bound to have left lookouts. We wouldn't stand a chance!"

"But if we stay in here," said Iggy, "we're doomed for sure."

"Maybe not," said Teggs, thinking hard. "I've got a plan, guys. It's incredibly risky – but I think it's our only chance!"

Chapter Eleven

CRASHING DOWN

Minutes later, Gipsy and Tute were building a barrier across the doorway to Keprish's lair, while Arx worked feverishly at the energy-screen controls in Keprish's altar.

Exhausted, Tute leaned against the pile of treasures blocking the entrance and watched anxiously as Skunch's T. rex army drew ever closer on the screen. The monsters were filling the narrow corridor beyond the bomb chamber like scaly rats in a drainpipe, scrabbling to break down the door. The sound of their fists and claws on the stone echoed eerily through the chamber.

"We can't rest, Tute," panted Gipsy, pointing to the hundreds of T. rexes still stirring opposite. "We've got to stop Ganster's lot getting out too."

"It's hopeless," sighed Tute, dragging Lord Ganster over to lie with his followers.

"Let's hope the roast-rifle will hold them off," said Gipsy, pointing to the weapon on the altar. "Hey, Arx, how are you getting on?"

"Almost there," Arx muttered, barely visible behind a huge tangle of wires. "I'm working as fast as I can."

"So's Iggy!" Teggs came rushing out from inside Keprish's rocket, covered in oil. "I can't help him any more – I'm not good enough with engines."

Tute grabbed hold of another heavy statue. "Then help me and Gipsy instead!"

Tense minutes dragged past as Teggs threw himself into the work with incredible energy, shoving every bit of furniture he could find up against the entrance

to the awakening T. rexes'
cramped quarters.

"There!" Iggy
staggered out of the
white rocket-ship as
it began to hum and
shake with power. "The
engines are working
again, but there's not much fuel left. I
don't even know if there's enough for this
nutty plan to work."

"If it doesn't, we're finished." Teggs
looked hopefully at Arx. "Are you nearly
ready?"

"Nearly." Arx didn't look up. "Or
nearly-*ish*, anyway."

A terrible crash sounded from the
chamber outside, followed by the blood-
chilling cheers of triumphant T. rexes.

"It's Brigadier Skunch." Gipsy had to
raise her voice over the rising rumble
of the rocket engines. "He's broken
through!"

Teggs looked at Iggy. "How long before the rocket's ready?"

Iggy pulled a face. "Not yet. Power's still building."

The next second, baying like giant scaly hounds, Skunch and his slavering troops appeared at the barricade. "So, the plant-eating scum-suckers still live . . . But not for long!" He started kicking at the statues and bric-a-brac barring his way, and his eager soldiers joined in.

"You should leave now, Skunch!" Teggs shouted over the ever-rising hum of the engines. "If you come in here, you'll reqret it."

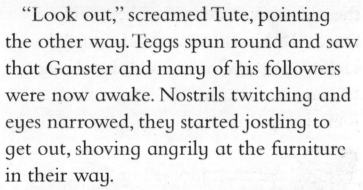

"Not as much as YOU will," Skunch yelled back.

"Look out," screamed Tute, pointing the other way. Teggs spun round and saw that Ganster and many of his followers were now awake. Nostrils twitching and eyes narrowed, they started jostling to get out, shoving angrily at the furniture in their way.

"What happened?" Leading his mob, Ganster tore the Scarab robes from his body. "Why me wearing such dumb clothes?" He glowered at Teggs and his friends. "Why me not smashing YOU?"

"Arx," Teggs cried, "how much longer?"

Arx bundled the wiring back inside the altar and started jabbing controls with his horns. "Thirty seconds!"

"That's all you've got left to live," roared Skunch as he and his troops broke through the barricade. At the same time, Ganster and his followers smashed their way out, yowling and howling over the angry whine of the rocket motors.

Gipsy fired the roast-rifle first one way, then another. A couple of T. rexes cried out or fell but the others kept on coming. "I can't stop them," she said helplessly. "There's too many."

"Power's almost up to maximum," Iggy reported.

"Finished!" Arx jumped up from the controls. "Get ready . . ."

"Stay close to the altar, everyone!" Teggs shouted as the raging 'rexes closed in, out for blood . . .

Then, suddenly, Teggs found himself flat on his back on the stone floor, pinned down by an invisible force. Gipsy, Arx, Iggy and Tute were there beside him, as if squashed by the air itself.

"You did it, Arx!" Teggs beamed. "You made Keprish's energy-screen prison larger – big enough to hold us all!"

"It was a good plan of yours, Captain," said Arx. "We can't move – but at least now we can't be got at, either!"

Baffled, Skunch tried to stomp on the astrosaurs – but his toes crackled with blue sparks and he was driven back. "OWW! My foot!"

"Hop it!" called Iggy.

Ganster's followers tried to bite and claw at the plant-eaters on the ground – but they had no more success than Skunch, sparks crackling around their teeth and fingers.

Gipsy breathed a big sigh of relief. "I never thought I'd be happy inside an alien prison!"

"It's definitely the best place to be right now," said Tute as the white rocket began to rise into the air, belching thick yellow smoke. "This is going to get messy . . ."

"Come on, you beauty!" hollered Iggy. "Show us what happens when a supersonic rocket meets a super-shielded pyramid roof . . . !"

Keprish's rocket suddenly shot upwards – and, with a deafening bang, crashed straight into the great stone ceiling. A massive explosion lit up the pyramid like a stolen sun as the shielding

short-circuited, and the heavy
bricks began to shatter
in a rain of rubble.

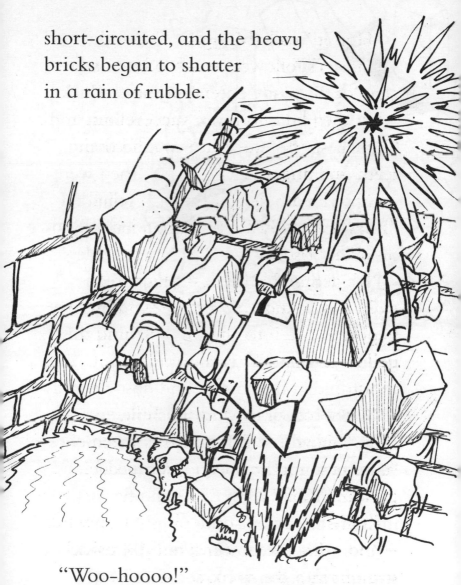

"Woo-hoooo!"
cheered Iggy as shards of stone bounced
harmlessly off their invisible prison.

But the
T. rexes were
not so lucky.
Yelling and
shouting,
they were
pounded
by falling
rubble.
Teggs
didn't
think the
deadly downpour would ever end . . .

But finally the smoke and dust cleared
to reveal blue skies and sunshine.

"It worked," said Teggs in amazement.
"The pyramid has been destroyed."

FF-ZZZZT! With a sizzling fizzle, the
invisible prison cut out.

"Boosting the power like I did made
the Scarab systems blow a fuse," Arx
explained, sitting up. "We can all move
again."

"Which is more than you can say for the T. rexes," said Teggs, looking around. Skunch, Ganster and their terrible armies were squished, squashed and half-buried by the remains of the pyramid.

"Hey ..." Keprish sat up on the altar, gazing around in wonder. "I can move again. I can actually move!" His one eye opened wider than ever, and his mouth stretched into a huge grin. "And my prison ... it's gone! I'm free, at last!"

"So you are," said Gipsy, trotting over

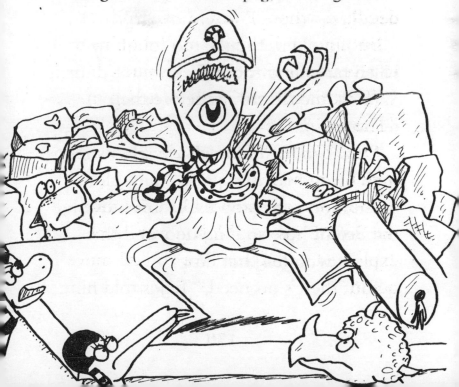

to join him.
"And guess
what, *I'm* free
too – to do
this!" WHAP!
She slugged him so
hard he went flying
off the altar and landed in a three-legged
heap in the rubble. Then she looked over
at Teggs with an apologetic smile. "Sorry,
Captain. It's been one of those days!"

"Keprish deserved it," Teggs assured
her. "Now, these T. rexes have taken
some blows but they're too tough to be
killed by falling rocks. We'd better disarm
Skunch and his troops before they
recover . . ."

"No," groaned Skunch weakly as Teggs
took away his laser guns. "Puny plant-
eaters, you can't stop us. Us must avenge
our defeat here so long ago, and the
T. rexes who fell that day."

"But there's no need," Teggs told him.

"We've already avenged that defeat for you! Look around." He pointed to the other T. rexes, slowly coming to their senses. "Your missing comrades are all still here – even Lord Ganster."

"Ganster?" Skunch stared in disbelief as the thousand-year-old T. rex struggled out from beneath a slab of stone. "Lord Ganster, be that you?"

"That be me," Ganster mumbled. "What happened?" He frowned and picked up the Scarab from the rock beside him. "Ahh. Me starting to remember this one . . . Him hurt my brain. Him made me do stuff me not want to do." As Keprish began to stir, Ganster squeezed the little alien tight. "Me teach him lesson he never forget!"

"That's a very good idea!" said Arx. "Keprish's prison here is finished – but for all the crimes he's committed against the T. rex race, he deserves to go to jail on *your* planet."

"And we caught him for you," Teggs pointed out. "You owe us big time, Skunch!"

"Me suppose you all be right." Skunch nodded slowly. "Us take him back to Teerex Major – right now."

"Or even sooner, if you can manage it," said Iggy, winking at Tute.

"And no trying to eat anyone or stealing treasure," Teggs added. "This is a plant-eater planet now – so push off or else."

Skunch looked around at his sorrowful troops with their lumps, bumps and bruises, and shrugged. "Yes. Us *will* push off. Us not need your dumb jewels. Finding lost T. rexes AND getting the scumbag what took them best treasure of all!"

"That's the smartest thing I've ever heard a T. rex say," Teggs declared as Skunch and Ganster led their limping followers back to their warcraft.

Gipsy noticed that Chef Sheff and his kitchen hands were back on their feet too. "Oi, Sheff!" shouted Skunch. "Us not eat plant-eaters this day, but need victory feast. What else you got?"

"Lots and lots of dung jelly!" said Chef Sheff happily. "With diplodocus toenails for pudding!"

Rubbing their tummies and saying, "Mmmmm!" the T. rexes staggered away.

"No! Help! Put me down!" Keprish had come round, struggling helplessly in Ganster's claws. "I insist you release me. It's not fair. I can't go to prison again . . ."

Gipsy giggled. "Oh, I think he can!"

"He was a great admirer of T. rex power – now he'll find out what it's *really* like," said Arx with satisfaction.

"And with that all taken care of," said Gipsy, "what about our holiday?"

"Holiday!" Teggs looked shocked.

"I forgot we were meant to be taking
a break."

Iggy sighed. "Starting with a hundred
mile hike back to the resort!"

"Our crew mates will come looking
and pick us up," Arx assured him.
"Though I'm not sure they'll believe our
story!"

"Not until we show them all these
lovely jewels," said Tute, peering about in

the rubble for more. "It's a shame to have trashed so many alien treasures – but at least *we're* still in one piece!"

"I'm sure there are plenty more hidden tombs and temples to be found," said Gipsy.

"And plenty more adventures too," said Teggs. "I'm looking forward to getting back on board the *Sauropod* and searching for them in outer space. But I really must admit – this has been the best holiday I've ever had!"

THE END

ASTRO PUZZLE TIME

THE T. REX INVASION
WORDSEARCH

A	E	G	I	O	T	V	S	U	C	F	G
Z	S	K	U	N	C	H	T	I	A	W	S
P	Q	T	D	J	L	C	E	M	R	K	A
W	Y	P	R	A	U	K	G	S	N	E	U
X	D	R	F	O	I	T	O	B	I	P	R
B	H	P	A	U	S	E	S	W	V	R	O
T	U	T	E	M	X	A	A	B	O	I	P
D	Y	F	Q	B	I	O	U	T	R	S	O
A	T	D	M	I	U	D	R	R	E	H	D
G	Z	O	E	U	P	A	U	L	S	R	I
J	O	S	P	A	C	E	S	H	I	P	L
I	G	U	A	N	O	D	O	N	G	K	S

ASTROSAURS   TUTE
STEGOSAURUS   PYRAMID
IGUANODON   CARNIVORE
SAUROPOD   KEPRISH
SKUNCH   SPACESHIP

Reading across, down and
diagonally, see if you can find
all the listed words in the
grid above...

ASTRO PUZZLE TIME

"Astro-Scramble"

"Evil alien Keprish has muddled all of these words. See if you can rearrange the letters and find the words. (Clue: they are all characters' names)."

SHIRPEK	
DORL STERNAG	
TEUT	
FECH HEFFS	

Answers:

1. Shirpek (Keprish)

2. Dorl Sternag (Lord Ganster)

3. Teut (Tute)

4. Fech Heffs (Chef Sheff)

ALSO BY STEVE COLE

Meet the time-travelling cows!

THE VIKING EMOO-GENCY

BY STEVE COLE

IT'S 'UDDER' MADNESS!

Genius cow Professor McMoo and his trusty
sidekicks, Pat and Bo, are the star agents of the
C.I.A. –short for **COWS IN ACTION!** They travel through
time, fighting evil bulls from the future and keeping
history on the right track . . .

In the year 878, England trembles under Viking
attack – but the deadly Danes are being snatched by
sea-monsters. What does this have to do with some
stolen zoo animals and a mad bull scientist from the
future? Only McMoo, Pat and Bo can find out!

It's time for action. **COWS IN ACTION.**

READ ALL THE

COWS IN ACTION

ADVENTURES!

JOIN THE SLIME SQUAD ON MORE
OF THEIR MISSIONS . . .

ABOUT THE AUTHOR

Photo: RebeccaJudge.com

Steve Cole has now written fifty books published by Random House Children's Books. As well as the hugely popular *Astrosaurs* and *Astrosaurs Academy* series, he is also the author of *Cows in Action* and *Slime Squad*, and the *Z. Rex* and *Tripwire* sequences for older readers.

Steve has also written lots of other books for different publishers, including several *Doctor Who* novels which have become UK bestsellers. He has also been the editor of fiction and non-fiction titles.

Steve lives in Buckinghamshire with his wife and two children. You can find out more about him at

www·stevecolebooks·co·uk

Visit **www.stevecolebooks**.co.uk for fun, games, jokes, to meet the characters and much, much more!

Welcome to a world where dinosaurs fly spaceships and cows use a time-machine . . .

Sign up for the free Steve Cole monthly newsletter to find out what your favourite author is up to!